my little life

When Shah Went Weird

Look out for more *My Little Life* titles:

When Ellie Cheated
When Scott Got Lost
When Geri and I Fell Out
When Dad Went on a Date
When I Won a Prize

And you can write to Tiff by e-mail at:
tiffany.little@hodder.co.uk

Jenny Oldfield

my little life

when Shah went weird

illustrated by Martina Farrow

Hodder
Children's
Books

a division of Hodder Headline Limited

Text copyright © 2002 Jenny Oldfield
Illustrations copyright © 2002 Martina Farrow
Cover illustration © 2002 Nila Aye

First published in Great Britain in 2002
by Hodder Children's Books

A Catalogue record for this book is available from the British Library

ISBN 0 340 85077 9

Printed and bound in Great Britain by
Bookmarque Ltd, Croydon, Surrey

The paper and board used in this paperback by
Hodder Children's Books are natural recyclable products
made from wood grown in sustainable forests.
The manufacturing processes conform to the environmental
regulations of the country of origin.

Hodder Children's Books
A division of Hodder Headline Limited
338 Euston Road, London NW1 3BH

A big thank you to the hundreds of kids I met
on school visits who helped me with ideas
for these books!

Wednesday, May 23rd

Your stars – It's a great day for chattin', chillin' and flirtin'. So go on, girl; enjoy!

Little by name, little by nature.

I mean, everyone else is growing up and out. They're five foot eight, with BOOBS. I'm five foot three and boobless. Tiny. Minute. Extremely small. And now I come to look closely, lopsided!!! Yikes!

A girl can get a complex about stuff like this.

Plus, I have ears that stick out like Dumbo the Elephant.

What boy could fancy me? Let's face it, I'm doomed to be a loser in LURVE!

Boo-hoo, poor me!

'Pull yourself together, Tiff!'

This is Mum's voice, over the phone, when I try to discuss my intimate problem. 'It's perfectly normal for a girl of your age to develop lopsidedly. It doesn't mean you're going to stay that way!'

'But people stare at me in the gym changing-room.'

'People-schmeople! You're just imagining it. Believe me, Tiffany, your school chums have other things on their minds than the size of your chest!'

'School chums'! Are we living in Enid-Blyton-Land, or what? Thanks, Mum, for that show of sympathy. And this is the mother who left my dad for some smarmy geek called Neil, who later went and dumped her. Or as she says, 'Neil and I are just taking a break to see how we both feel.' Yeah, really!

'Bye,' I say, in a big huff. Bang go my chances of surgical enhancement for my size 30AA chest when I reach the age of thirteen.

Bang goes my dad in the kitchen. Bang-bang-bang. Bob the Builder's at it again. Can he fix it? No, he can't!!!

Well actually, he can, because that's his full-time job. Being a builder. But he takes his pace from Sammy Snail. Like, an inch a day.

He's been working on our new kitchen for months now, knocking out windows, making new ones, putting up walls, re-routing the plumbing, modernizing the lighting . . .

Sad fact is, we have no running water and our only cooker is the microwave plugged into a socket in the telly room. There's brick dust everywhere.

Big question: how can a great writer write great stuff whilst living in a muck-heap?

Gorgeous George, our English teacher, says you need a quiet room all of your own. No distractions. Flowers in a vase on the window sill, books lining the wall, your desk looking out over green trees and a softly winding river . . .

Not bang-bang-bang from Bob.

'That noise is giving me a headache!' I yell downstairs.

'Whooo-ooo!' Scott scoffs. ''Ark at 'er!'

'Shurrup, Scott!' Scott the blot on the landscape, Scott the Blot.

'Careful, Dad. Tiff's got PMT!' he yells. He just learned about it in Biology, I bet.

Dad emerges from the hole we call the kitchen. He's wearing ear-muffs. 'What's empty?' he asks.

Scott laughs.

I don't.

Dear Anna Mae,
I hear that in America you can sue your parents
for not making a good job of bringing you up.
Can we do this in England yet? If not, why not?
  T. Microscopic (Upper Piddleford)

(Best use an alias and leave no clues to my real identity.)

Dear Ms Microscopic,
Is that your real name? You may have bad parents,
but you live in a charming village in the Cotswolds
that I know well, having spent family holidays
there when I was a girl. Many kids live in not so
nice places with awful parents. So quit whining.
  Anna Mae, Agony Aunt to the Stars

P.S. Luckily, we don't live in America, where everybody sues everyone for everything.

P.P.S. You do mean the Upper Piddleford up the hill from Lower Piddleford, Wenburyshire, don't you? There's a pub called the Dick Turpin, which does good bar meals.

Dad stops bang-banging and answers his

phone. Bet it's Carli. She usually rings about sixish. 'Hi, Ross. What kind of a day have you had? Blah-blah. Fancy a quick drink down the Snail and Grapefruit?'

Which is partly why our kitchen never gets done. Dad's in LURVE with my art teacher, which is weird, even though I did play Cupid to get it kick-started. Weird, as in, how d'you act when you see your dad's girlfriend giving your best mate a detention?

Carli (alias Miss Ganeri): Fuschia Allerton, why haven't you handed in your homework?
Shah (alias Fuschia): Please Miss, I left it at home.

Carli: That's the fifth time this term I've heard that excuse from you. Don't you think you could come up with something more original?
Shah: Yes, Miss. The cat was sick over it.

Which was when she got given the detention. For being disrespectful. Shah claimed she was provoked.

'What's that mean?' Geri asked while practising her backhand smash against the sports' hall wall.

'Ganeri asked for it,' Ellie explained. Ellie never attempts a backhand smash, in case she breaks a fingernail.

Which is why it's weird for me. I mean, whose side do I take?

They all look at me; Shah, Geri and Ellie, and I just shrug. Privately, I wonder what's up with Shah? She likes art, so why isn't she doing her homework? And why is she suddenly dressing like this:

i.e. like an American cheerleader. Pom-pom-diddy-pom, marching along! It's not big and it's not funny. Ellie won't be seen dead with her looking like that.

That's it; Dad's stopped banging for the day. He clunks a bit while he ditches his tool in the metal box then carries the box out to the van, which has a sticker on the back window saying, 'No tools are stored in this van overnight'. Hah!!

Soon it'll be a shower, a quick dose of after-shave and then meeting Carli in The Hen and Parrot.

It's my turn to walk the dog, and Bad-Breath Bud knows it. He's just galloped upstairs trailing the lead after him.

Walkies-pant-pant!

'Urgh, Bud, go away!'

Jump-jump-scrabble-pant!

'I mean it, Bud. I'm busy!'

Pant-pant-walkies!

'Yuck, Bud, you stink! Dad, where's the Odor-eeze?'

'Dunno. Scott, where's the Odor-eeze?'

'Uh!' (Translation: Naff off!)

Big Bro probably squirted the dog's bad-breath

spray all over himself in a desperate effort to impress the women. He never reads labels. He once ate a whole bag of doggy-chocs by mistake. Personally, I think he needs to wear glasses.

'Bye, you two!' Dad yells from the front door. 'Oh, and Tiffany; that dog needs a walk!'

Silence from me.

Dad slams the door behind him.

Bud breathes all over me. I give in and take him to the park.

Thursday, May 24th

 *Your stars* – *This week's full moon suggests that it's time for you Leo gals to examine certain friendships. Leos really look out for their mates, but it seems that one of your friends isn't returning the favour. Don't let her take you for granted. Tell her how you feel. She won't wanna lose you, so she'll have to mend her ways.*

Bang-bang-bang downstairs.

I can't concentrate.

Sound-torture. It's like the drip-drip-drip of a tap, only we don't have running water. Sweating

14

under the glare of a bare light-bulb. *'Ve have vays und means of making you talk, dumbkopf English spy!'*

Bang-bang-swearword-bang!

And I'm trying to write a new song for Ellie's band. They want a fast and funky one. The words have to smack you right between the eyes. I thought of a title – *Here Comes the Future.*

> *It's a new day dawning,*
> *A brand new start,*
> *What a day to be born in,*
> *Listen to your heart.*
>
> *Here comes the future,*
> *Gotta make my way.*
> *Here comes the future,*
> *Come what may . . .*

Nah, that doesn't work.

Bang-bang. C'mon, Carli, ring him! Drag him away from his pipes and U-bends!

> *It's me, I'm calling*
> *To say I'm falling*
> *In love with you.*

Can't help it,
Here comes the future
And it's here to stay . . .

Nah!

No LURVE stuff needed. Think Ellie, think wannabe –

Sleek white limo and designer labels,
Sipping cappuccino at the very best tables,
A sunshine yacht in the south of France
Baby, you really gotta grab your chance!
Cos I tell you,
Here comes the future,
And it's you-oo-ou!

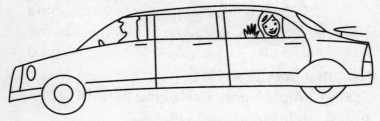

Hmm. I can see Ellie singing that.

'Bye, you two!' Dad calls up the stairs.

I guess I missed the Carli call and the shower. But I do detect the lingering whiff of Brut.

'Scott, it's your turn to walk the dog!'

'Uh!' (No translation needed.)

Bang goes the front door.

'Gerroff, Bud!' from Big Bro's room.

Scott knows I'll dob him in if he just kicks Bud out into the back garden. Unless he blackmails me with half his week's paper-round money.

'. . . Bud, you stink!'

Bud got Scott to take him down the park, then something weird happened.

First, I heard Bud come lolloping back and start slurping water from his dish in the hall.

Scott did his usual grunting apeman act, came upstairs and flopped down in front of his telly.

I was just finishing the third version of *Here Comes the Future* – the girl gets every single thing she wants . . . the silk sheets, the diamonds, the famous footballer – when the front door opened again and Dad came in.

I went out on to the landing. No Carli.

'What did you forget?' I asked.

'Nothing. Go back to bed.'

'I'm not in bed. It's only eight o'clock.'

'What? Oh yeah. Whatever.' Dad took his jacket off, fetched his tools from the van and soon started banging again.

Then, brring-brring at the front door, which I scooted down to open.

Carli's standing there in a tight white T-shirt and skinny denims. She's wearing the chunky silver and turquoise necklace that she always wears to school. Being an art teacher, she wears arty stuff. 'Is your dad in?' she asks.

'Da-ad!'

He appears covered in dust, carrying a spanner.

'What happened to you?' she asks.

'What happened to you?' he replies.

'We said seven at the Rat and Parrot,' she reminds him, not wasting any words.

'No, we said the Slug and Lettuce,' he corrects.

My head's going from right to left like I'm watching a tennis match. Scott is hovering on the landing. Talk about being able to cut the atmosphere with a knife!

'It's Thursday, it must be the Rat,' she counters, low and hard over the net. Thirty-fifteen.

'But we made it the Slug because we didn't want to do the quiz at the Rat,' he objects. Thirty-all.

'*You* didn't want to do the quiz,' she insists. Forty-thirty.

'I said I did, but you obviously weren't listening.'

'That's not good enough!' Game to Carli.

'Watch out, I'm gonna walk the dog!' Scott can't stand any more. He lumbers downstairs and grabs Bud's lead. Two walks in one evening. The poor dog nearly dies of shock.

I'm thinking of offering to make a cuppa to break the silence.

'Well, never mind,' Carli mumbles at last. She manages a fake smile. 'For a moment back there, I thought I'd been stood up!'

'I rang you, but I didn't get a signal,' Dad explains. 'Then I guess I thought you'd switched your phone off because you'd decided to dump me.'

I wince. I think Dad chose a bad word – 'dump'. Too strong. He sounded a tad bitter.

Carli laughs but she doesn't mean it. 'Are you coming then?'

'To the Rat?' He looks down at his dusty jeans.

'Yes, the Rat!' she insists. 'Get a move on, or we'll miss the quiz!'

I text Geri: 'D & C had row. Embarratastic!!!'
Then Ellie: 'D & C fell out. Wtch ths space!'
Then Shah: 'Mega fight btwn D & C. Ouch!'

They all texted me back.

'Grwn-ups! Wld y'blve it!'
'Dtails tmrrw, plse!
'Dnt thnk u shld goss abt Ms Gnri!'

Since when was a goss about a teacher a crime? That's what I mean; Shah is turning really weird.

Anyway, the house is empty and I'm scribbling. Since I won the prize in the national writing competition, I've been inspired. Currently working on a novel about a girl called Shelley whose parents are going through a painful divorce. Lots of autobiographical stuff. Mr Fox always says we should write about what we know. And I know about divorce, believe me!

Friday, May 25th

Your stars – *Thrills and spills are on the cards for Leos later this month. But don't rush out and buy a South African safari – the wildlife is coming to you!*

Huh, the only wildlife I'm in contact with is the fleas on Bad Breath! I think they jumped into my bed. Now I've got great red itchy bites all up my leg. 'Don't scratch them!' Mum warned when she dropped some anti-itch cream off on her way home from work.

Too late. I already scratched. You try not to.

Ugly, or what? I look like I've got some dreaded disease, to add to all my other issues about the way I look.

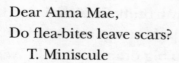

Dear Anna Mae,
Do flea-bites leave scars?
    T. Miniscule

Dear Tiny T,

Only if you scratch.

Anna Mae, Agony Aunt to the Stars.

Said hi to Carli during art.

She took me to one side and said, 'What was wrong with Scott last night?'

I said, 'Take no notice. He's like that all the time.' Apeman.

'So it's not just me that he doesn't like?'

'No. He hates everyone.'

Big Bro is gonna be a major character in my autobiographical novel. He's gonna go off the rails big-time – probably drugs and everything. (Must bring home Drugs Info leaflets from the library, to get my facts straight.) He's gonna steal cars and end up in prison.

Carli nodded and went back to teaching.

'What did she say?' Ellie hissed. She never misses a thing.

'Nothing. It was about Scott.'

'Huh.' Not interesting. 'I wondered if she mentioned the F-I-G-H-T.'

I shook my head. 'I think it blew over. Dad came back from the pub in a good mood.'

Sniff from Ellie. No big drama after all. Weird;

Dad's love life is a big talking point between me and my mates.

Like, at break, after the art lesson. I told them about Scott blanking Carli big time.

'So what's new?' Geri said. 'You can tell he doesn't like your dad having a girlfriend.'

'Yeah, any girlfriend!' I agreed.

'Well, it is a bit . . . freaky,' Ellie chipped in. She was only half listening, and reading my lyrics to *Here Comes the Future* at the same time.

'What's freaky?' I didn't like that comment.

'Y'know; it should be Scott having a girlfriend, not your dad at his age. Or maybe that's what Scott thinks anyway.'

'Yeah, the peabrain,' Geri muttered. She's not into boys. Not even Nic Heron. If you can't smash it with a tennis racket or a hockey stick, Geri's not interested.

'Who thinks my dad should be going out with Carli?' I demanded, trying to include Shah.

'Me,' Geri said.

'Me,' Ellie added, humming a tune.

'I think he should ditch her.' Shah voted against. No explanation; nothing. She just swanned off before the bell went, leaving a dirty great silence behind.

'What d'you mean; ditch her?' I squeaked during lunch break. I mean, I was shocked. What was wrong with my lovely dad going out with my cool art teacher?

Shah flared up straight away. 'Do I have to spell it out? It's a bad thing. It won't work out. Full stop!' Her brown eyes flashed, she was practically spitting out her words.

'What got into her?' Ellie asked, all wide-eyed and astonished.

Shah had delivered her verdict then flounced out of B Hall.

'She has to go see Mr Maths White before next lesson, Lisa Sharman told us.'

'Whoo-oo, Fuschia Allerton's in deep doo-doo!' Squealer picked up the ball and ran with it. 'Who's been a naughty girl, then?'

Maths White is our Head of Year. It's bad news if you have to go to his office.

'She never mentioned it,' Geri frowned, trying to ignore the Piglet.

'Stay in after school for three and a half years!' Adam Pigg imitated Maths White's poncey voice. 'Pick up litter in the playground for ever!'

'Your hair's too long, your skirt's too short!' Dom Skinner joined in. 'I sentence you to life imprisonment!'

'Leave it out,' I muttered. I'm getting really worried about Shah. She's totally different – like she's had a brain transplant. She used to be kind. Yeah; kind and gentle and kind of dreamy. Sure, it could get on your nerves sometimes, but you knew she would never harm a fly.

'Life is great!' Mum insisted. She called to see Gran Little, who had suddenly landed with her overnight bag.

'It's Bank Holiday weekend,' Gran had announced. 'I had to escape the gaggles of kiss-me-quick tourists!'

Gran lives by the seaside. She likes to keep an eye on Dad, now that he and Mum have split up. The tourist thing is just an excuse.

Gran also lives to bake. So she'd arrived with tins full of choccy cake and flapjacks. The first thing she'd done was ring Mum and invite her over for tea.

'Life's really good.' Mum said it twice, with a cheesy grin.

'Now tell me the truth!' Gran is not a subtle person. She's always dead up front.

'No, really!' Mum's bottom lip quivered. 'I've joined a gym.'

'Puh!'

Waste of money. Silly women prancing about on running machines. What's wrong with a twenty-mile cycle ride out in the fresh air? Gran didn't have to say it, but that was what she meant by, 'Puh!'

'And an art class,' Mum went on. 'We've got this interesting teacher – he's Rumanian, a real womanizer!'

Rumanian-Shoomanian! Gran sniffed.

'There are lots of interesting people in the group.' Mum was babbling while Gran poured the tea. 'There's somebody who must be at least your age.'

'Ancient!' Gran crowed. 'I like your cheek, Gina Little!'

Mum raised a smile. Genuine this time. 'Ooh gosh, I needed this cup of tea!' she sighed. She kicked off her high heels and curled her legs under her.

Then Dad came home from work. He must have seen Mum's car parked outside, but instead of coming in and saying hi, he skirted round the back and avoided her.

'Tiffany, go and see if your dad wants a sandwich and a cuppa.' Gran carried on as if nothing was the matter. As if Mum and Dad hadn't split up and everything was hunkey-dorey. Talk about sticking your head in the sand!

'Gran says, d'you want a sandwich?' I told Dad. He looked tired as he slung his toolbox into a corner of the bombed-out kitchen.

'No thanks, love. Tell her I'm off out for a meal later.'

'Mum's here,' I muttered.

27

He looked at me. 'I know.'

'You could just say hello.'

He nodded and geared himself up. Then he went and poked his head around the telly room door.

'How's things?' he asked Mum.

'Great,' she said. 'I was wondering if you'd come across my Braveheart video anywhere.'

'Nope.'

'OK, never mind. I'll buy a new one.'

And that was it. Classic.

Dad went upstairs and ran the shower.

Saturday, May 26th

Your stars – *The spotlight is on money. You're in a spend-spend-spend mood, but remember, it's not your birthday for ages yet. How about getting a Saturday job and earning some dosh?*

I'm not old enough for anything except a dreaded paper round. Getting up at six and having your clothes shredded by a fierce version of Bud is pants!

If I was Ellie, with all the dosh swimming

around at her place, I wouldn't have to worry.

But then again, I'd have to have Mr Smart Suit Shelbourn as my dad. No, on second thoughts . . .

Nic came round this morning to hang out with Scott. They did BOYZ STUFF – internet etc – then watched a preview for the World Cup.

Gran gave them flapjacks.

'It's never little Nic Heron, is it!' she cried. 'It can't be! The last time I saw you, you and Scott were playing in a paddling pool in the back garden in a little pair of striped swimming trunks!'

Nic blushed.

I went dizzy at the thought of Nic in a pair of swimming trunks. Nic is fit. F-I-T. I think he's getting fitter as Scott gets grosser. And the nice thing about him is that he doesn't seem to notice. Girls can tell him he's drop-dead gorgeous right to his face and he just grins and walks away. Me, I just worship from a distance.

Anyway, he was in the house, eating flapjacks and watching telly!

Be cool! I kept telling myself. But a look from Nic's blue-grey eyes is like an electric shock. My heart goes into overdrive. I get sweaty palms.

Dear Kylie (I'm fed up with the sort of reply I would get from Anna Mae),
I'm in love with my brother's best mate, but he doesn't seem to notice me. What can I do?
  Tiffany

Dear Tiff,
This is a common story, and there are ways to handle it. Why not find out about his fave music and buy him a CD? Put on that spesh outfit next time he calls. If all else fails, drop a heavy hint that you'd like him to take you out. Remember, this is the 21st Century!! Good luck with your flirtin' and snoggin'!
  Kylie

P.S. Whatever you do, don't ask your brother to tell him how you feel!

Boys and football. Boys and the World Cup. It's all they ever talk about.

Scott: What are the chances of Oxley being fit to play in the first match?

Nic: Dunno, but I reckon Erskine will play it close to his chest. He'll want to keep Argentina guessing.

Scott: A knee injury like that is tricky. Oxley's done it before, to the other knee. It took him six weeks to get back to full match fitness.

Nic: England can't afford to leave him out. He's the backbone of the defence.

Scott: On the other hand, Erskine might want to save him for the match against France.

Nic: Yeah, we're in a tough group.

Yawn-yawn! It's in every newspaper, on every TV channel. We've got football on the brain. Will Oxley be fit? Will Aaron Miller score in his first game for England? Has Embley's left big toe really been blessed by the Pope?

World Cup Fever.

People are flying flags outside their houses. The England team song has reached number 1 in the charts.

'We'll beat the world,
Oh yes we will.
We'll win the Cup,
In for the kill . . .'

This time next week, a billion people will be watching twenty-two men in shorts kick a leather ball around a square of grass.

Mega-yawn.

Texted Ellie: 'Ftbll is pnts!'

She texted me back: 'R u at hme?'

Me: 'Yep.'

Ellie: 'Wll b thr soon.'

Texted Geri: 'Ftbll is pnts!'

Geri: 'R u mad? Am glued 2 TV!'

Texted Shah: 'Wanna cme 2 my hse?'

Shah didn't reply.

Decided to leave the boys to their preview and work on my book until Ellie came round:

That's when Ben finally lost it.

It was his dad's business who he went out with, but Ben found he couldn't be in the same room with the woman who was standing there with a sickly smile, asking him to call her 'Mum'.

'You aren't my mother!' he yelled at Emma, his face crimson with fury. 'You're just some woman I hardly even know!'

Ben, that's enough!' his dad warned.

Ben turned on him. 'And you!' he ~~yelled~~ screamed. 'You couldn't care less what happens to Mel and me. Just as long as you're OK with your new woman and your new life, it doesn't matter what's happening for us kids!'

Frank's temper snapped. Swearing hard, he swung his fist at Ben, who ducked. Then the boy hit back. He connected with Frank's jaw, but it didn't happen like it does in the movies. No way. Frank looked shocked but stayed upright. Ben's knuckles hurt like crazy.

From the doorway, Melanie cried out. 'Stop it both of you!' The sight of her father and brother fighting sent her white with shock.

Only Emma seemed to stay in control. She pulled Frank away from Ben, then picked up a ~~table~~ chair that had been knocked over. 'Give him time to get used to it,' she told Frank. 'It's probably all come as a bit of a shock.'

But Ben knew that he would never get used to living with a stranger. Why should he? He was fifteen years old. He would move out, live in a squat, manage fine by himself.

Ben's character: hot-tempered, secretive, shy. Clever, but always in trouble at school.

Frank's character: strict, doesn't listen, a police sergeant. His wife left him for another man.

Emma's character: hard-faced, ambitious, tells lies. Puts on a false face for Frank.

Melanie's character: forced to be strong and act older than her age (12). Keeps the family going after Mum walks out without even leaving a note. Forced to miss school and look after Frank. Secretly, she dreams of going to dance school, but the dream looks like it's never going to become a reality.

I'm going to call it *After You've Gone*, and part of it is going to be written as if Mel is keeping a diary where she 'talks' to her absent mum:

'Mum, I'm missing you loads. I don't know why you left, but please come back. Today was awful. Ben and Dad had a big fight. Ben walked out. I feel terrible. Everything is going wrong and I don't know who to talk to. If only you came back, everything would be fine.'

The big mystery will be what did actually happen to the mum. Either:

1. She walks out because Frank was beating her up and she can't stand any more. She goes to a battered wives' shelter and gets help to rescue the kids from their violent dad.

2. She finds someone else but can't bring herself to tell the kids. Eventually she misses them so much, she comes back and takes them away with her..

3. Frank loses his temper and kills her. He buries the body and the police eventually find it. They arrest Frank, who is sentenced to life in prison. Ben turns sixteen and is old enough to take care of Mel. Mel goes to dance school.

Creative flow interrupted by Scott, Nic and Bud in the garden.

'Goal!' Scott croaked. His voice is taking forever to break. Sometimes he squeaks like Minnie Mouse.

I looked out to see Bud with a football scarf tied around his neck and a striped woolly hat on his head. The boyz had put him in goal while they took penalty shoot-outs. Very funny, ha ha.

'Goal!' Nic yelled.

Poor Bud didn't stand a chance.

'Heron's magical left foot finds the back of the net yet again!' Nic cried. He jogged back towards the house to let Scott line up the ball for another penalty. Glancing up, he saw me watching from my bedroom window. Like an idiot, I ducked out of sight.

Ouch! I banged my head on the bookcase as I dived.

'Goal!' Scott crowed after his next shot. 'Little lines England up for a historical victory over the World Champions of '98!'

'Rrrruff!' Bud harried the ball across the garden. He dribbled it with his nose, bending it like Beckham.

'The goalie's left his goalmouth unprotected!' Scott gasped. 'This could turn out to be a very costly mistake!'

Zooming in, he took the ball away from Bud and slammed it between the goalposts. It was the most exercise Scott has had all year.

Then Ellie showed up. 'Hi, Nic!'

Ellie in a micro skirt with fake tan on her legs. Ellie with her blonde hair shining in the sun. Total babe.

'Hi, Geri!' Scott leered. Cradle snatcher!

She glared at him. 'Get it right, can't you? I'm Ellie!'

She's only been coming to my house since we

were four years old. Not long enough for Apeman to work out who she is, obviously.

Ellie floated up the path and into the house like a super-model. 'That Nic Heron is yummy!' she sighed as she flopped down on my bed.

I was still rubbing my head, wondering if the bookcase had given me brain damage.

So Ellie picked up a mag and flicked through. 'It says here you can tell bags of stuff about a person just by looking at the shape of their faces. Like, a bumpy hooter means your life is full of ups and downs. But if your nose is straight, you're loaded and hitched up with a yummy man.'

'Says who?'

'This article.' Ellie never needed any encouragement to stare into the mirror, which was what she was currently doing. 'Dimpled chin equals drama queen. Pointed means born leader.'

'What about big ears?' I muttered, sidling up to the mirror.

Ellie read on. 'Pointed lugs means you're a brainbox. Big lobes means good luck. Wide holes equals top chick . . .'

'What about overall big – like ginormous?'

Ellie lost interest and dumped the mag. 'Dunno, doesn't say.'

She fiddled with her hair for a bit, then sighed. 'I'm bored!'

'Hey, look at this!' I dragged her to the window. Shah had just turned up with her sister, Skye, and a lad I didn't know.

'Who's that?' Ellie hissed. Gorge-boy-alert! Six feet of toned muscle, dark hair and grey eyes.

I shook my head.

'Let's go see!' Ellie was down the stairs and out in the garden before Gran had time to say, 'Would you like a cup of tea?'

'Hi, Tiff, hi, Ellie!' Skye came in quick with the introductions. 'This is Callum.'

Callum has a square chin, small ears, and full lips. His eyebrows are bushy (a minor fault), and his lashes are long and thick. I don't need to read any magazine article to know what that says about him. He's one gorge hunk! Swoon! Sigh!

'Callum's from Glasgow. He plays in a band,' Skye said proudly.

'Hey, I sing in our school band!' Ellie piped up, and she was off, telling him about their material, and how they wrote a lot of their own stuff (no mention of me), and how they had a gig coming up on Bank Holiday Monday, and would Callum still be around, cos if he was, then he could come and watch her.

Once Ellie gets going, there's no stopping her. This has it uses, since it allows me to stay in the background and gawp all I want.

And gawping at Glasgow Boy put me in a much better mood. I even forgot about my sore head.

Tea came, and so did choccy cake. Bud wolfed a chunk of it down before we realized he could reach it on the garden bench. Scott almost strangled him with the football scarf.

'Chocolate is bad for dogs,' Shah announced. It was the first time she'd opened her mouth. Then she made a big show of looking at her watch, as if she had a million better things to do.

Ellie grabbed her and dragged her inside. 'Who's the hunk?' she demanded. 'What's he doing with your sister?'

'That's Skye's boyfriend, obviously! She just showed up with him.'

'Yeah? So they're still an item?'

Shah shrugged.

'C'mon, give us the goss! Where did they meet? Are they like, y'know – living together?' Ellie wanted details.

'Haven't asked.'

Ellie was gobsmacked. 'You haven't asked! Y'mean, you haven't had time yet?'

If Skye and Glasgow Boy had just arrived at the Allertons' house for the holiday weekend, perhaps Shah hadn't had chance to dig the dirt.

'No. I mean, it's none of my business.' With a toss of her dark hair, Shah escaped outside.

'How snotty was that!' Ellie yelped. Being snubbed by Shah was worse than a *schmack* in the face.

I rolled my eyes.

'Now, now,' Gran broke in. She must have picked up some of the bickering about Callum. 'No falling out, kiddos. Not on a nice sunny day like this.'

Bless! Gran in her pink flowery trousers and dazzling yellow bandanna. She hates it when people row. She likes sunshine and happiness, and love and peace.

'I'm outta here!' Ellie announced. Ms Drama Queen flounced off to talk with Geri behind Shah's back.

Meanwhile, back at the ranch . . . i.e. out in the garden, Skye and Shah were discussing the bad effects of junk food. E numbers and all that. Glasgow Boy was being ignored by Scott and Nic and looking pretty left out. I smiled at him, but no way could I think of anything to say.

(Wish I wasn't shy. Would give anything to be in-your-face and confident like Ellie. Dad once mentioned that he finds it hard to walk into a pub sometimes — everyone turning their heads to stare makes him curl up inside. So I s'pose that's where I get it from.)

Then it struck me; there was a pretty antsy situation here:

Nic fancies Skye. Skye doesn't know he fancies her. Nic doesn't know that Skye has a new boyfriend. Nic must be shocked and devastated to see Callum with the girl he adores.

I couldn't work out who to feel sorry for at first, but then I came down heavily on Nic's side.

Poor bloke, he's heartbroken and having to put on a brave face, still messing about with Bud and Scott.

'Convenience foods are a major threat to the

health of a whole generation of young people,' Skye declared. She studies psychology at university. I like her, but the fact that she's dead brainy scares me.

'Chocolate never did me any harm,' Gran objected. 'And you see so many anorectic girls around these days . . .'

'Anorexic,' Shah muttered.

I glared at her.

'. . . so many anorectic girls, I just want to feed them up with good old fashioned home baking!'

Skye and Shah could see they were getting nowhere. They hung around for a bit, then decided to go into town. Shah didn't bother to ask me if I wanted to come. I stood at the gate and watched the three of them jump on to the next bus.

Nic was beside me, staring longingly at Skye's back view.

So I screwed up my courage to open my mouth and spoke to the most gorgeous lad in the whole universe.

'How about a piece of chocolate cake?' I gabbled.

Sad, or what!

A once in a lifetime chance, and I sound like my Gran!!

Sunday, May 27th

*Your stars – **Love**: You're feeling a bit wobbly, so try not to be too self critical, especially when it comes to recent lack of boy interest. That's all about to change for the better; a kiss that's been on the cards for ages is about to happen!*

__Life__: You thought you knew your best mate inside out. You're going to be shocked by what she tells you, but do your best to be understanding.

I hate it when your star forecast leaves you hanging in mid air. Now it's buzzing round my head non-stop. I bet it's to do with Shah. On the other hand, I do know that, bottom line, horoscopes are a load of manure! So why do I read them every day? I'm gonna stop; I really am!

Bad news; Gran mentioned Mum's name in front of Carli. The reaction was not good.

'What?' Gran protested after the whole thing

blew up. 'Aren't I even allowed to say that Gina had rung about Tiffany's next visit without getting my head bitten off?'

'You didn't get your head bitten off,' Dad told her. 'Anyway, you can't blame Carli for being a bit insecure about the fact that you and Gina still get along like a house on fire.'

'So I'm supposed to delete my daughter-in-law from the picture, am I?' Gran was on her high horse by this time.

'Ex-daughter-in-law,' Dad said.

'Oh, so the divorce came through, did it?'

Dad tutted and walked away. They were both sulking big time.

This is my version of the actual event:

Carli came round for coffee. Gran introduced herself while Dad was upstairs in the loo. They made polite conversation about school and art.

'I'm thinking of taking up life-drawing,' Gran said.

I'm thinking, Don't mention that Mum has joined a class! Already I got the feeling that Gran was not going to give Carli an easy ride.

'You should,' Carli replied. 'You'd probably get a lot out of it. Tiffany, for instance, is very artistic. It probably runs in the family.'

'Ah yes, but Tiff gets that from her mother's side.'

Ouch! Yep, she'd deliberately brought Mum into it. I saw Carli smile weakly.

Dad came down.

'Ross, I was just telling Carli here that Gina is the artistic one. Did you know she showed me a sketch which she'd done at art class when she was round here on Friday? It was brilliant! Oh, and by the way, she rang to say she'd pick Tiffany up an hour late next weekend.'

By this time there was a frosty silence coming from Carli. No doubt about it; she was feeling dead left out. So I scooted upstairs while Carli went with Dad into the kitchen, pretending to take an interest in the building work. But Belfast sinks and integrated appliances are NOT what they actually talked about. I know; I could hear through a hole in the floorboards.

'It sounds like Gina calls or drops in just about every day.' Carli opened up the subject.

'There's a lot to organize, to do with the kids,' Dad pointed out.

Long pause, then Carli said, 'Are you sure it's just that?'

'Meaning?'

'Meaning, it seems like Gina doesn't want to let go.'

Try talking to Dad about anything complicated, like emotions, and you lose him in a flash.

'Don't talk so daft,' he scoffed. Then straight away he said sorry. 'I didn't mean it like it came out,' he explained. 'I just mean that it was Gina who kicked me into touch, not the other way around. So why on earth would she still want to hang on after she was the one who walked out?'

'People do,' Carli insisted. 'A lot happens under the surface, without ever being said.'

Dad was quiet after this. He made coffee, and he and Carli chatted in a friendly way. But she soon went home.

Then Dad had a go at Gran for mentioning Mum, and Gran stuck up for herself.

Happy families. OK, so no one's killing anyone and burying bodies under patios. But it doesn't have to be melodrama. More nickety-nickety, people chipping away, ruining a situation.

Watch this space.

Ellie texted me:

   'S. hs rlly dn it ths time!!'

I texted back:

   'Wht nw? Rng me on lnd line.'

Ten seconds later, the house phone rang.

'D'you know what she's done!' Ellie squeaked.

'Who, Shah?'

'Who else?'

'No, tell me.'

'She's only backed out of tomorrow, that's all!'

Tomorrow. The bank holiday gig. Ellie's big night.

'We're only rehearsing at my house last night when Skye, Callum and Lady Stick-It-Up-Your-Jumper turn up! Callum's really cool; saying nice things about us, how great Dom is on keyboard, and how good Lisa and me sound on your new song.'

'*My* new song?'

'Yeah, we're gonna use *Here Comes the Future* tomorrow. Callum thinks it sounds really gutsy. Anyway, he's giving us a few cool tips about our dance moves, when Shah comes out with it. "This isn't my kind of music!" she says, loud enough for everyone to turn and stare. "I like the small indie labels, not this commercial stuff."'

'Since when?' I gasped.

'Since last night!' Ellie scoffed. 'I couldn't believe I was hearing it!'

'I know,' I agreed. Up till this point, Shah has been writing the music for a lot of Gemini's songs. She's been really into it, like the rest of us.

Ellie flounced around my room, picking up my hairbrush and flicking it through her hair. Then she turned to towards me and looked me in the eyes.

'Honestly, Tiff, I'm worried about Shah. Don't you think she's turned totally weird?'

'OK, I'll go and see her,' I promised at last.

It was the only way I could calm Ellie down. I mean, Ellie comes across as mega confident, but Shah had really upset her. And she was getting on my nerves too.

'Hang around!' Geri advised, when I phoned her and told her the latest. 'Don't go steaming in straight away. Wait until we all get back to school.'

'But that'll be too late to make Shah change her mind about tomorrow night,' I pointed out. 'That means a lot to Ellie.'

'Well, fools rush in where angels fear to tread,'

she quoted, sounding like her dad. 'And don't say I didn't warn you.'

I asked her if she fancied coming along to Shah's house with me for back-up.

'Sorry, no can do.'

'Why not?'

'I'm playing in the semi-finals of the Junior Tournament at the tennis club.'

Whack. Bash. Slam. What you see with Geri is what you get.

So I ended up going by myself earlier this afternoon.

And who do I bump into going up the Allertons' drive but Mum! She was looking great – hair a bit messed up, smiley face, tight T-shirt and loose trousers and DKNY trainers. I'd KILL for those trainers!

'Oh Tiff, I feel fantastic! I've just had a reflexology sesh with Fuschia's mum. Now I feel as if I'm floating on air.'

Mrs A is into all that stuff – foot massage, feng shui, pilates – people pay her loads of dosh to learn how to de-stress, and Mum has become one of her biggest customers. Rescue remedy, sticking needles into you, and cleansing your aura. You name it, Mrs Allerton does it. And charges plenty.

'Remember to close your toilet-seat lid before you flush' is one of the ten commandments according to the feng shui bible. Shah told us about it on Friday without cracking a grin.

We were all in the girls' loos, giggling about something. When Shah said that, I doubled up and laughed until my stomach hurt. Don't ask me why, I just did.

'It's true!' she insisted.

That's how weird she is these days.

'I think Shah closed the lid on her sense of humour and flushed it down the loo!' Geri said afterwards.

'She used to be so . . . NICE!' Ellie complained. 'Always a bit arty and weird, I guess, but never Miss Nose-in-the-air!'

So it had built up and come to a head over the gig, and there I was trotting round to her place to sort it out.

Mugsville!

'Have you seen Shah?' I asked Mum.

51

'No, but listen, I hear from your Gran that things aren't going very smoothly for your dad right now.'

'Leave it out, Mum!' No way did I want to play piggy in the middle.

'Your gran's worried about him. She rang me this lunchtime. I could hear him bang-bang-banging away in the background, taking out his frustrations on that stupid kitchen!'

'Yeah well it's not for you to worry about any more,' I pointed out. 'You just have to let him get on with it. It'll get finished one of these days.'

Mum tutted. 'I'm not talking about U-bends and plumbing, and you know it.' She didn't have to mention the name Carli Ganeri for us both to understand.

'Mum!'

'Sorry, Tiff. It's not fair of me to ask, is it?'

'No, definitely not!'

Just go, walk out the door!
If it's true what they say,
You don't love me any more!

The words of an ancient pop song rang inside my head. 'I will survive!'

'Sorry,' she said again. Her face fell. She looked like a lonely old woman who has to get her fix from reflexology, and I suddenly felt sorry for her.

Whoosh-whoosh. My feelings are pushed about like I'm sitting on a park swing.

'Sorry, Mum. You'd better talk to Dad if you really want to know what's going on.'

She nodded. 'What're you doing tomorrow?'

'Watching the carnival, then going to watch Ellie's band.'

Carnival where I live = a procession of lorries decorated as ships, fairy grottoes and Telly-tubby Land, with kids from local playgroups all dressed up. There'll be a brass band and a steel band, drum majorettes, and two massive shire horses pulling a brewery cart. The police will close the main street to traffic and we'll all buy ice creams and helium balloons. Then we'll shuffle along en masse to the fair on the rugby ground. Kids will puke up their ice creams on the waltzers.

When I was six it was magic. We won a prize for the best decorated float, all dressed up as fishes and octopuses, as if we were swimming around in a giant tank.

(Octopuses/ octopii/ octopi? Dunno. The dictionary doesn't say. It's radius/ radii though.)

I was a giant squid squirting black ink from a water pistol.

Wicked.

'Well, have a nice day,' Mum said quietly, then she got into her car.

Seven years ago, she was the one who made my

squid costume, natch. It's simple stuff like that
that gets to you. Like old photos of us all on the
beach. And the wedding album, when they
looked dead young and happy, with Gran Little
in a fuschia pink hat and purple suit, and Gran
Jackson in cream, with pointy gold shoes. In
most of the pics she's holding Scott, who was two
years old at the time. He looks dead cute, which
just goes to prove how photographs do lie.

I said bye to Mum and rang Shah's bell.

'Hey, Tiff!' Skye came to the door. 'Have you
come to talk Shah out of her bad mood?'

I paused in the doorway. 'Is she still in one?'

'Deeply depressed!' Skye told me. 'I diagnose
a serious case of early adolescent angst.'

angst, noun. (use is often ironical) a morbid
anxiety, especially about the state of the modern
world.

Thanks, dictionary!

'Is she in her room?'

Skye nodded. 'Being about as much fun as
a wet weekend. We suspect a food allergy,
an intolerance to wheat or dairy products.

They're gonna put her on a special diet.'

So we were back to the dreaded E numbers. I nodded and made my way upstairs.

Knock-knock. No reply. Just music droning out under the door, slow and whiney.

Knock-knock. 'Shah, are you in there?'

'Go away, Tiff. I'm busy.'

Well, that made me mad. I pushed open the door and saw her sitting cross legged on the floor, with the blinds down and surrounded by those little tea-light candle things, all flickering away.

'What d'you mean, you're busy? You're only sitting here listening to naff music!'

'This isn't naff music,' Shah sighed. 'This is Kareena.'

'Never heard of 'em.'

'No, well you wouldn't.' She closed her eyes and swayed in time to the dreary rhythm.

'Shah, what's got into you? Why are you being so horrible to us?' I was wading

in big time. That's what we Leos do.

She opened her eyes. 'Show me the rule that I have to be nice.'

'What!'

'Why do I have to pretend to be something that I'm not, just to make you, Ellie and Geri feel OK?'

'B-b-but, we're your friends!'

She sighed again. 'Things change. People move on.'

I was gobsmacked. This was so not like the Shah I knew.

'Now, if you don't mind, Tiff, I want to listen to the rest of this CD.'

Bank Holiday Monday, May 28th

 *Your stars – You're so darned confident that mates sometimes forget that you have a big squishy heart. If they carelessly hurt your feelings today, let 'em know the damage they do.*

Boo-hoo. I mean, genuinely, boo-hoo-hoo!

I came home from Shah's place yesterday crying my eyes out.

'Don't take it to heart,' was Gran's advice.

'It's not your problem,' said Mum on the phone.

Dad gave me a fiver for the carnival.

'I'm never gonna speak to Fuschia Allerton ever again!' Ellie swore.

We met up at Geri's house at 11.30 a.m., to get dressed for the day.

I took three tops and two pairs of trousers.

'Wear the pink trousers with the turquoise top,' Ellie told me. 'And borrow my Nike trainers!'

I tried it all on, and I have to admit, it did look cool.

I mussed up my hair and gelled it, making sure that the fringe was spiky and pulled straight down over my eyes.

'Go easy on the glitter eye shadow,' Geri warned.

'Yeah, save that for tonight,' Ellie agreed.

She chose a striped top with a sequinned American flag on the chest for Geri, teamed with an A-line frayed denim skirt.

'A skirt?' Geri moaned. 'Can't I wear trousers?'

'Nope, the skirt goes with the top. You look cool,' Ellie insisted.

And she did.

Ellie wore a rose-pink strappy top with cream cotton lace trim. Her floaty skirt skimmed her knees. Total babe, of course.

'No contest!' Geri grinned.

'Cinders, you shall go to the Carnival!' I waved my magic wand and we left in our golden carriage.

Everyone was there. I mean, everyone.

It was a sunny day so the whole town turned out. Mums, dads, kids in pushchairs or being carried on shoulders. Grandmas with grandads in wheelchairs, young couples sitting at tables in the pavement cafés. The streets were hung with bunting, recorded music blared from loud-speakers. Ice cream vans tinkled out tinny tunes.

Then the procession started.

Oompah-oompah! The brass band led the

way. A big man on the bass drum, wearing a leopard-skin tunic, a tiny man on the trumpet. A beefy man with a moustache blowing away on the French horn. They were all dressed in bright red uniforms with gold braid and shiny brass buttons.

'Where did they dig them up from?' Ellie giggled.

'From some army regiment,' I told her.

Left-right, left-right. Oompah.

Then the kiddywinks came on the decorated floats. You had your Star Wars and your Lord of the Rings. And your Harry Potters and Winnie the Poohs. Isn't it funny how a bear likes honey . . .

'Aah!' Geri cooed. 'Remember when we all used to do that?'

'Yeah, you were an elf!' Ellie reminded me.

Nightmare! 'Let's not talk about it!' I pleaded.

One little Harry Potter put his hands over his ears and cried for his mum.

Boom-boom-oompah! The band played on.

Then there were grown-ups walking along in fancy-dress. Women doing step-aerobics in their silver leotards, hairy men from the local rugby team dressed in drag.

'It's all for a good cause,' I heard a grandma

explain to her tut-tutting husband. 'All the proceeds go to charity.'

'You still wouldn't catch me dead wearing bosoms and high heels!' he grumped. 'In my day, it would never 'ave 'appened.'

Tring-ding-a-ling! A steel band followed the Lily Savage lookalikes. Musicians in wild, wicked costumes made of feathers and frills, wearing big flowered head dresses and ginormous smiles. Trill-tring-a-ling.

'Cool!' we all said, salsa-ing along. We followed the steel band down to the field, where they were planning to judge the floats and some men from the RAF were gonna land their parachutes. We met up with all the kids from our class, including the dreaded Squealer and Chucky.

'Cor, Geri, I didn't know you had legs!' Chucky leered.

'Naff off,' she told him, no messing.

'Tiff, how about coming to tonight's gig with me?' Squealer wheedled.

I poked two fingers down my throat and made puking noises.

'Very nice!' Squealer laughed.

If you think Adam Pigg has feelings to hurt, you can think again. He was only asking in order to wind me up.

Then we saw Scott and Nic. They were hanging around by the waltzers. Scott was wearing his England shirt. How sad is that?

As fate would have it, as they say in trashy novels, Skye and Callum were riding on the waltzers. They stepped off right by Scott and Nic and brushed by without seeing them. Callum had his arm around Skye's waist, love's young dream. Wow, that must've hurt Nic plenty. He's a classic case of unrequited love.

I didn't see him after that, though Scott stuck around to watch the parachutes land.

'I was hoping someone would break something,' he muttered to me after all twelve had landed safely in trails of blue and red smoke.

'Sadist!' I said darkly.

'Watch it, Tiff's swallowed a dictionary again!' Geri warned.

'Sorry – not!' I'm used to them giving me a hard time over the words I use.

'C'mon, let's go on the waltzers!' Ellie said.

D'YOU WANNA GO FASTER? . . . YEAH!

We had a break at four, to let Ellie get ready for the gig. Which gave me time to write this and think a few things through:

1. I feel I looked OK today, hurrah! I can get away with bright colours because my hair's dark and I'm looking pretty tanned already, even though we haven't had much sun. I even managed to forget about my big ears and lopsided chest.

2. I do feel mega sorry for Nic.

3. Can't leave things as they are with Shah. Something's wrong with her, and I can't work out what it is. It's like she's put up this big wall around her and she keeps us out by chucking insults.
Wonder what to do next?????

LOOKING IS ALL YOU CAN DO

A poem by Tiffany Little, dedicated to Nic Heron

Looking is all you can do
Though your heart is broken in two.
You gave her one part
Right from the start
But looking is all you can do.

Her eyes dance, though not for you
Her lips laugh, her love is true.
You stand to one side
Nowhere to hide
When looking is all you can do.

Try again, find someone new
What's the good of feeling blue?
Tears fill your eyes
A long goodbye
Since looking is all you can do.

This would make a good song. Shah could write the music.

COULD . . . if only she'd stop acting weird!

Monday evening

Funktastic! The best! One superspesh night for Gemini! I'm so excited I can't sleep. I mean, if a singer in a pro band says you're gonna make it, you have to believe it!

That was Callum Hendry talking to Ellie during the interval, giving her the lowdown on Gemini's performance.

'Listen man, let me link you up with my manager. Hire a studio and make a demo tape, send it to me and I'll make sure Micky hears it.'

Geri and me were hearing all this, backstage with the band after their first set. Heather (Miss Westlake) and Gorgeous George (Mr Fox) were listening in as well.

'I never heard a school band as cool as you guys,' Callum told them. 'And you look cute too. All the ingredients are there.'

Ellie was looking stunned. She'd sung mega well. Especially *Here Comes the Future*. And her dancing was steptastic!!!

'You know how to get the audience on your side,' Callum went on. 'You make good contact, instead of just standing there onstage and not making any connections.'

'We chose the kids partly for their outgoing

personalities,' Heather explained. 'Plus their talent, of course.'

The boys in the band – Callum (talk about coincidence!), Dom and Marc – wore sheepish grins. The girls were fizzing.

Ellie spoke for everyone. 'Thanks for watching us!'

'No problem. As it happens, I was wondering if you'd mind me singing along with you during your second set.'

'Mind!' Lisa echoed. 'You mean, you wanna be our surprise star guest?'

Callum grinned. 'Something like that, man.'

So he did.

The audience went wild, stamping, shouting and screaming.

Even the boys.

Callum sings with a high voice mixed in with a croaky gravel. Ronan Keating, eat your heart out! He sounds as if he's singing specially for you and you alone.

Angel! Angel on the sidewalk . . .

It was one of my songs. I nearly died and went to heaven.

I stood with Skye at the side of the stage and got a mega view. We sang along and danced our socks off. The lights half blinded us and the sound system wrecked our eardrums, but hey, who cares!

Like I say, funktastic!

'We'll send you that demo!' Heather promised as she shook hands with Callum after the gig.

'Yeah, and maybe you can all come up to Glasgow to see Mickey,' he said. He was fighting off the fans at the time.

'Gemini will be on telly yet,' Gorgeous George said. We were all grinning like idiots. I was so happy for Ellie, I wanted to hug everyone.

And she deserves it. She works mega hard on her singing. It's totally, one hundred per cent what she wants to do.

A vision of the future: Ellie is Posh Spice of 2010. She lives in a mansion and drives twenty cars. *Hello* magazine pays her squillions to take photographs of her wedding to a soccer superstar. Me, Geri and Shah are her bridesmaids. In an

interview with a national newspaper she says how important her mates are. 'I could never have done this alone,' she confides. 'The four of us have been friends since we were little. We're gonna stick together, no matter what!'

That's if we make up with Shah.

Yeah, Shah. She wasn't at the gig, so she missed all the excitement. But she did show up with her mum at the end. Mrs Allerton had arrived to pick up Skye and Callum from the stage entrance of the King's Hall. Shah hung around in the semi-darkness while Callum escaped from his fans. I only caught a glimpse of her, but I could swear she'd been crying. Her eyes were red and puffy.

'Hay fever?' Geri suggested, when I passed this on.

But Shah never had a sniffle of hay fever in her life.

'No, she'd been blubbing,' I said.

1.30 a.m. – finished this and went to bed.

Tuesday, May 29th

Your stars – Perhaps your dream boy is right under your nose and you haven't noticed him. You might find you're more willing to talk to him when your friends aren't around.

Dad's in a bad mood.

Gran's in a bad mood.

Scott's in a mega bad mood (so what's new?). He's flinging things around.

Living in this family is beginning to feel like an extreme sport.

'I know when I'm not wanted,' Gran said.

'Don't be silly, Mum.' Dad was wolfing his toast.

'It's true,' Gran sniffed. 'And y'know, the last thing I wanted to be was one of those interfering old busybodies who doesn't know when to keep quiet!'

'You're not. Don't be daft.'

'Gerroff!' Scott snarled at Bud, who was chewing his trainer.

I ate my cornflakes in silence. Crunch-crunch.

Gran put the tops on everything and brushed away crumbs. It's a bad sign when she gets supertidy. 'I was only trying to help.'

'Mum, put a sock in it, will you!'

'It's a pity when I can't talk freely to my own daughter-in-law.'

Uh-oh! Not that again.

Scott wrestled Bud for his shoe. 'Ergh, look at this slobber!'

'Mum!' Dad got up from the table. He grabbed his van keys. 'I'll see you later, OK.'

Scott and I collared him for our lunch money while Gran chuntered under her breath.

Dad banged out of the house, leaving unfinished business.

'Gerroff, Bud!' Scott yelled about the other trainer.

'I'm off!' I said. 'See you later.'

'No, kiddo, you won't.' Gran gave me a fixed, sad little smile. 'I've outstayed my welcome, so I'll be packing my bag and leaving.'

Ouch! 'Take no notice of Dad,' I begged. 'Whatever he's been saying, Scott and I want you to stay. Don't we, Scott?'

'BUD, GERROFF MY TRAINER!!!'

'Thanks, Tiffany, you're a sweetheart. But it's best if I leave Ross to sort out his own troubles; I realize that now. And listen, I'll give you a ring when I get back home, make sure that everything's calmed down at this end.'

I got big hugs, then left.

What does Gran mean, Dad's 'troubles'? And what exactly was the row about? That's what they do; give you half the story and leave you hanging. Grown-ups!

'And Callum say he's gonna get us a professional, full time manager!' Ellie was telling anyone who would listen, which was half our Year group. 'Heather says we can hire a studio with the money we made at the gig last night, and make a demo tape!'

'Wow! Cool! Bonza! Wow!' Everyone was well impressed.

'Gemini is gonna make it!' Ellie promised.

She's got stars in her eyes.

Geri and I hung around the outside of the gang. Geri looked at me. 'Y'know; just maybe!' she murmured.

Bright, shiny Ellie singing on TOTP, twirling and glittering her way to the top. Blonde babe stepping out to mega success.

'More than maybe,' I grinned. 'After last night, I'm a believer!'

We shuffled into registration, where Miss

Hornby soon pummelled us into shape.

'Ellie Shelbourn, you may be the latest pop sensation to hit the bedazzled nation, but not while you're in my tutor group, you're not!'

'No, Miss Hornby.'

'So I would ask you not to gossip whilst I'm taking the register.'

'No, Miss Hornby. I mean, yes, Miss Hornby!'

'And while I'm on the subject, Ellie, since when was pearlescent blue nail varnish part of school uniform?'

Ellie blushed and muttered under her breath.

'I take it, that was, "Never, Miss Hornby!"' our beloved teacher sneered. She went on with the register until she came to Shah.

'Fuschia Allerton.'

Silence.

Miss H looked up at Shah's empty seat. 'Anyone know anything about Fuschia?'

'No, Miss,' we all murmured.

Only that she's gone totally weird. But we didn't tell Hornby that.

Then, in our art lesson, Carli collared me and asked me outright about Shah.

'Tiffany, what's wrong with Fuschia?'

'Dunno. Must be sick.' When I'm nervous, I

talk like a dork. State the obvious in words of one syllable, uh-uh-uh!

'No, I mean what's wrong with her generally? She used to be one of the pupils I really enjoyed teaching, but she's gone off lately. I wonder, is there a problem at home?'

I shook my head.

'C'mon, Tiff, you can tell me; off the record if you like. I'm just curious as to the reason. Y'know, no homework handed in, no piece ever finished in class. And she used to be so keen.'

Yeah, Shah is definitely the arty type, normally.

I shrugged. Dunno. Search me.

Carli's used to me and my apewoman replies, so she persisted. 'Shah wasn't at the gig last night, was she?'

'No. Well yeah, but only at the end.'

'I didn't see her.'

I flashed Carli a look, not realizing that she'd been at the King's Hall herself. And not with Dad, as far as I knew. Well, definitely not with Dad. He'd come to pick Scott and me up in his old work clothes.

'I was helping George and Heather on the door, and I certainly didn't notice Fuschia.'

'She came at the end,' I repeated. End of conversation.

I texted Shah during lunch break: 'Wht's th prob? U sick? Poor u. Txt me.'

She didn't reply.

I came home to an empty house. Gran's gone. Bud had gone crazy and chewed his leather lead to shreds. Gross.

Made tea in the microwave – baked spuds, cheese and beans. Pudding was leftover choccy cake  from Gran's visit, heated, with a splodge of whipped cream on top. Yummy.

Dad's been plumbing. I love the smell of the solder stuff that you melt to make joints in copper pipes. Tomorrow we will have water coming through the new taps. I've been sniffing and watching for a while. 'Hey, Dad, watch out, you're developing plumbers' bum!'

'Never!' He hitched up his jeans rapido.

'No, just kidding!' I made him a coffee and watched some more. 'What did you and Gran argue about?' I asked after a while.

'Oh, nothing,' he sighed.

'Was it about Mum?'

'Kind of. Did your gran ring to say she'd got back safely?'

'Yep. So what was the row about exactly?'

Dad saw that I wasn't gonna let him off the hook. He put down his soldering iron and sipped his drink. 'Mum means well, but she's not the most subtle of people.'

Loud Gran in her bandannas, riding her yellow bike. Gran putting her size 4s into her mouth!

Dad sighed again. 'Your gran's purpose in life at present is to get me and Gina back together, and she doesn't care who knows it.'

I nodded, guessing that he was meaning Carli here. Gran had definitely not been subtle with Carli.

'She thinks she can wave a magic wand and make everything OK again, but it's not that simple.'

My turn to sigh. Why isn't it that simple? I want to ask. Couples do get back together, and things work out. Fairytale endings.

'Like I say, she means well. But she pushes too hard.'

'She was upset,' I murmured.

'I know. I'd better ring her.' Dad wandered off into the hall with his coffee. 'Oh, and by the way, Tiff . . .'

'What?'

'Don't go getting up your hopes, just because your gran has a bee in her bonnet.'

'What d'you mean?'

He looked at me with a sad smile. 'Whatever Mum thinks, there's no way that Gina and I will get back together, OK.'

Wednesday, May 30th

Your stars – *You might not be feeling on top form, so take it easy today. And remember, you're the best so don't let anyone tell you otherwise.*

'Tiffany, you're a sad git!'

This was Scott, after I refused to take Bud for a walk when it was Scott's turn. And that was only the start of what's turning out to be one of the worst days of my life. I thought I was going OTT with the plot for *After You'd Gone*, but believe me, real life is twice as complicated!

Still no Shah in school today, and she's not texting us back. Ellie texted her this morning, then Geri tried this afternoon. When we try to ring her on her moby, it's always turned off.

But the big news is to do with Carli.

Carli and Georgeous, to be exact.

I'll write that again:

Carli Ganeri and Gorgeous George Fox, my hero.

Gob-smacking! In fact, maybe I got it all wrong.

It went like this: I was trying to text Shah (again), in the library during lunch break. I'm tucked away behind the Apple Macs, minding my own business. George is across the room, leafing through a book from the Literary Criticism section. But he's glancing around as if he's expecting someone.

I'm dithering over whether to pop out from behind the computers to discuss my auto-biographical novel with him. Yes-no, yes-no, when in shimmies Miss G.

'Oh hi, George! Blah-blah, George! George-this, George-that!'

He grins a lot and doesn't say much.

I'm looking on in disbelief. If this wasn't the

school library and I didn't know that Carli and my dad were a definite item, I would say she was flirting with him big time!

'I enjoyed Monday night,' she tells him, implying more than she's saying outright.

'Me too.' He's self-conscious, but sounding pleased.

'Thanks for inviting me back to your place,' she says in a sexy voice.

Back to *his* place??!!

(I'm writing it down and making myself believe it.)

'I enjoyed it. We'll have to do it again,' George says, implying more than he's saying.

I'm red to the roots of my hair. My pulse is racing. What about Dad? I'm thinking. I'm like a mother tiger, ready to spring out and defend her cub.

'I didn't plan it,' she says.

'Me neither,' he replies.

Their heads are getting very close together.

I'm about to clear my throat and put in an appearance, since I couldn't bear to witness an actual snog between my dad's girlfriend and my fave teacher.

But then the bell goes and they spring apart.

Selina Minto, the librarian's assistant from Year 9, suddenly races out of the tiny office and almost bumps into George. What's the betting she's been earwigging too? Soon it'll be all around school.

I'm still hiding behind the hardware, shaking like a leaf.

'Shall I tell D-D-Dad?' I ask Geri and Ellie during maths.

I've never stammered in my life before. I must be shell-shocked.

'Quiet, Tiffany!' Mr White bellows without looking up. I swear that man's got inbuilt radar.

'No way!' Ellie and Geri hissed back.

'Tiffany, I won't be warning you again!'

(Get your radar MOT'd!)

'It'll only cause a big bust-up!' Ellie tells me.

'Let them work it out between them,' is Geri's advice.

'Tiffany Little, I'm putting you in detention on Monday of next week,' Mr W informs me, without even pausing in his ticking and crossing.

Chucky sniggers, so he lands in detention with me.

Double bummer.

'But if I don't say anything, it'll feel like I'm lying to him,' I pointed out on the way home from school.

Ellie didn't get this. 'How come? I mean, how can keeping quiet equal lying?'

Geri did get it. 'It's like a sin of omission,' she explained. Her family are all religious. They talk about things like that.

'Yeah, right. Like I'm deceiving him by not telling him that Carli's two-timing him.'

'And if you tell him, you spoil his day,' Ellie came back at us.

'And anyway, maybe you got it all wrong. Maybe George and Carli are just good friends.'

Chicken that I am, I clung on to this excuse as a reason to go home and act as if nothing had happened.

But I spent the whole time not looking at Dad, who brought back a Thai takeaway.

'What's on telly tonight?' he asked in the middle of his Kaeng Pa.

'Footie,' Scott mumbled through his noodles.

Slurp-slurp.

'Which match?'

'Brazil versus Germany. Nic's coming round.'

'I'm off,' I said, heading for Mum's flat, which would be a footie-free zone. And to be honest, I couldn't bear the sight of Nic's broken heart.

'You seem a bit down,' Mum said to me after I'd only been there a nano-second.

I gulped, to stop myself blurting out the Dad-Carli-George love triangle. I mean, all I needed was for Mum to get involved. 'It's Shah,' I sighed.

'Tell me all,' Mum invited.

So I did.

'Shame!' Mum sympathized. 'I remember a time when I was younger than you, about ten, I think. Anyway, the last year of junior school. I had this best friend called Gina Matthews, who was born in the same hospital on the same day as me, and of course we had the same first names.'

I must have heard this story a hundred times, but I let Mum tell it again.

'We were best mates, went everywhere together, like your little gang. Then one day, I got a note from Gina saying she didn't want to be friends any more, because she'd decided to go and be friends with Sara Briggs, whose dad ran a chain of fashion stores and who had loads of trendy clothes.'

'Not nice,' I sympathized back.

'I was heartbroken. I took me ages to pick myself up and find someone else to go around with. I felt like I'd been screwed up like a piece of scrap paper and thrown in the bin!'

'But it's not as if Shah's gone off with anyone else,' I pointed out, curled up on Mum's posh and immaculate pale blue sofa. 'She just stays in the house and refuses to answer messages. When we do see her, she just throws insults at us.'

Mum agreed that this was weird. 'I'll tell you what I'd do. I'd take the bull by the horns and go round and see her!'

'I already did that, remember, and it didn't work.'

Mum thought for a bit. 'Try again,' she told me.

'But what if she bites my head off – again?'

'Then tell me, and I'll have a word with her mum. Between us, we should be able to get to the bottom of this.'

I agreed on the plan. 'Because I am really worried about her,' I sighed.

'I can see that it's getting you down.' Mum gave me a hug.

That and a million other things. Gran, Dad, Scott . . . the list goes on and on. 'I'll go round there first thing tomorrow,' I promised. 'See if I can drag her into school with me.'

Thursday, May 31st

Your stars – You're one step closer to landing that cutie. Don't stop now . . .

I threw the mag in the bin. ('Find out how fab the day's gonna be with our star gazer, Mystic Mel.')

'Bud, leggo!' Scott was screaming at the dog as I left the house half an hour early and took the detour round to Shah's place.

It was raining buckets, the traffic was a nightmare and I was feeling pretty stressed out by the time I arrived. But first I ran into Skye and Callum, hoodies up, rucksacks and guitar cases sitting in puddles beside them, standing at a nearby bus stop.

'Hey, Tiff!' Skye called me from across the street.

I dripped over to talk to them. 'You going home to Scotland?' I asked.

They nodded. 'Back to the haggis,' Callum kidded.

We chatted for a while about Ellie's band and demo tapes etcetera. Then the bus appeared around the corner.

'Gotta go!' Skye grabbed her rucksack.

'How's Shah?' I gabbled.

'Fine. Why shouldn't she be?'

Everything was happening fast-forward as the bus squished to a halt.

'Where is she now?' I asked.

'Oh right, I get it!' Skye hopped on to the bottom step after Callum. 'You wanted to walk into school with her!'

I nodded.

'Too late. She left about ten minutes ago.'

'How come?'

'She's been setting off early this week, to get to the art room and finish her project, or something.'

Swish! The door closed behind Skye, who waved and blew me a kiss.

Splatter! The bus sprayed puddle all over me as it set off.

I dashed to school and waited for Geri and Ellie to show up.

'Listen to this! Shah's been lying! She's been pretending to set off for school, just like normal. Her family thinks she's been in all week!'

'Y'mean, she's been bunking off!' Geri gasped.

'Oh my god!' Ellie's eyebrows shot up, her jaw dropped.

I nodded. 'Skye told me. But the thing is, what's she actually been doing all day if she's not been in school?'

'And how's she gonna get away with it?' Geri wondered.

Ellie didn't agree. 'Well, she has so far!'

'What's she doing all day?' I repeated.

'No wonder she doesn't answer her phone,' Ellie breathed.

We were huddled in the main entrance, with kids and teachers streaming by.

'Bunking off!' Geri said again.

We were all so gobsmacked that we didn't bother to keep our voices down and didn't notice Gorgeous George listening in until it was too late.

'Who's been bunking off?' He stepped into the middle of our huddle and demanded an answer.

Of all the teachers in the school, George is the one you can talk to. He's dead kind and interested; you sort of know he's on your side.

But even so, all three of us clammed up.

The First Commandment: Thou shalt not dob in a friend!

'Come on,' George insisted. 'If you won't tell me, I'll have to work it out.'

We kept our lips velcroed together.

George waited a few seconds. 'It's not rocket science,' he said quietly. 'We're talking about Fuschia here, aren't we?'

No reaction from us.

'Listen, if Shah's bunking off, we need to let her parents know.'

By this time, we were all wishing we'd bitten off our own tongues rather than get into this lousy situation. Well, I know I was. And Georgeous wasn't enjoying it any more than we were.

He shook his head and sighed. 'Come on, let's take a walk along the corridor to the Year Head's room.'

Aagh, no! Not Mr Maths White. Nightmare. Let me out of here!

But the bottom line was, George is a teacher. It's his job to make sure pupils come to school. 'This is worse than pulling teeth,' he told us, as he marched us along. 'But painful as it is, it has to be done.'

We ended up outside Mr White's door while George went in and explained the situation.

'I'll kill Shah when I get my hands on her!' Ellie hissed.

Geri sighed. 'Thanks, Tiff, for telling us something we didn't need to know!'

'What was I s'posed to do; keep it to myself?'

'Yeah – no. Sorry,' Geri muttered. She stared up at the anti-drugs poster on the wall.

'Come in, you three!' Mr White commanded.

George stood beside him, looking uneasy. We all avoided eye contact and gazed at the pukey purple carpet.

'I hope you realize how serious this situation is,' Mr W began in that tone of voice which says, 'We're all going to be sensible and discuss things like grown-ups'.

We concentrated on dumb insolence, which Geri is the best at. I'm usually too stressed out to keep it up for long.

'Tiffany.' Mr W turned to me. 'Mr Fox tells me that you know more about this situation than the other two.'

I huffed and puffed, exercising my right to remain silent.

'If you know for certain that Fuschia is

truanting, you must give us all the information.'

Mr Maths White has big hands. That's what I noticed when he leaned across his desk towards me, his hands clasped in front of him. He has a very deep voice and that radar stare.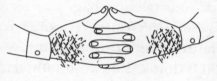

'It's for the best,' George added, playing Mr Nice.

Mr Nasty lost patience. 'Come along, Tiffany, I don't have all day!'

It was like facing the firing squad. If Ellie and Geri hadn't been to either side of me, I would've caved in then and there.

'Listen, your little friend, Fuschia Allerton, is already in all kinds of trouble,' Mr Nasty went on. 'Can you explain, for instance, why the school has had no reply to the FOUR letters I sent home with Fuschia, requesting an interview with Mr and Mrs Allerton?' He held up four fat, sausage fingers. 'Four!' he repeated. 'All in sealed envelopes and handed over personally by me into Fuschia's safekeeping!'

How stupid is that! What's wrong with a first class stamp?

'No?' Mr W prompted. 'Well, my bet is that those letters never reached their destination, and that they remain screwed up in the bottom of your friend's bag.'

Silence from us. George is looking like we're letting him down big time. We are. We're acting like dorks. But we totally hate Mr Maths White and would rather die than help him. Besides, we're in a state of shock about Shah.

'Fuschia may look sweet and innocent,' Nasty Man went on, 'but she doesn't fool me. I have a list of complaints from her teachers as long as my arm.'

He has apeman arms – long and hairy, attached to those massive hands.

Mr Hairy counted off Shah's crimes on his fat fingers. 'Never hands in homework, never finishes an assignment, can't concentrate in class, doesn't wear correct school uniform . . .'

'The point is,' George interrupted, 'we're worried about Shah, and we need to sit down together and work out how to help her!'

'We're way out of our league here!' Geri decided.

'They can't be serious!' Ellie kept saying. 'Shah wouldn't do the stuff they're saying!'

I was too shattered after our interview with Apeman to add anything.

'And she kept it all secret!' Geri pointed out. 'Not a word to any of us.'

'No wonder she's been acting weird!' Ellie was just taking it all in. 'And I've been so wrapped up in my own stuff that I didn't even notice what she was going through!'

'Yeah,' I agreed. What kind of mates were we? Why didn't she trust us? Mega loads of guilt came crashing down. 'Her mum thought it was E-numbers!'

Shah had been going through all this totally alone.

'Listen, let's think this through.' Geri made us concentrate.

It was lunch break, and the rumours about Shah had spread like a forest fire.

She'd run away from home. Her mum and dad were going to appear on telly and make an appeal for her to come home. She'd been kidnapped/ abducted by a weirdo/ murdered.

'We have to get to Shah before anyone else does,

91

and warn her about what's happening! That means we go straight from here and find her!' Geri is the practical one. 'Where the heck is she hanging out all day when she should be here?'

Ellie and I shrugged. 'Town?' I suggested.

'Listening to music in Virgin Megastore?' was Ellie's idea.

'All day?' I asked.

'We could try Virgin first,' Geri decided. 'Then how about the bookshops, and maybe the library.'

'And the art gallery,' I added. 'And maybe Warner Village.'

We did all this, in the order I've just written.

Virgin, Borders, library, then bingo, art gallery!

I'm racing to get this down, which wrecks the suspense, but hey, diaries aren't like novels; they're not meant to be read by anyone else. I just want to get the facts down straight.

The art gallery is where we finally caught up with Shah. It's an old building with big stone pillars at the entrance. You go up some steps into a marble hallway where a double life size naked man stares down at you. There are massive paintings on the wall of pink angels sitting on fluffy clouds.

'Where do we start?' Ellie asked, avoiding the naked man with her gaze.

'How about the Pre-Raphaelite gallery?' Geri had studied the floor plan and decided for us. So we scooted up some shiny stairs into a room full of pictures with long haired women looking pale and ill and men in grey armour looking serious.

'Wow!' Ellie gasped.

A man in a uniform standing at the far end of the long room gave us a warning look.

Closer to us, a group of French tourists were being given the gallery tour in French.

'Spooky!' Geri whispered about a picture of a woman with a long neck and white hands. Her eyes were closed and she seemed to be dreaming, while a red dove hovered nearby.

'Shah's not here. Let's go!' Ellie urged.

But then the French group moved off, and there she was sitting on a little bench, sketchbook in hand.

Shah sitting there sketching!

Totally focused on what she was doing, as if she was alone in the world.

Ellie panicked. 'What now?'

The gorilla in the uniform was giving us more black looks.

Geri admitted that she hadn't thought this far ahead. She turned to see what I thought.

'Don't look at me!'

'It's down to you, Tiff,' Ellie decided.

'How come?' I was backing out of the gallery, shaking my head.

'You know how Shah ticks,' Geri said. 'You're both the arty type!'

'Yeah, you have to go and tell her what happened.'

Like; Hi, Shah. We just went and blew your cover. The Thought Police are on to you. There's no escape! 'I can't!' I hissed.

'Wimp!' Geri challenged.

I nodded. 'One of you two will have to do it!'

'No, you!' Ellie grabbed me and pushed me forward.

Gorilla Man frowned and took a step towards us.

'Go on!' Geri insisted.

So I tiptoed forward, thinking that soon Shah was bound to turn round and see me. But I got right up to her, could see this amazing pencil drawing of the portrait she was copying, before she realized there was anyone else in the room.

'Tiff!' She closed her sketch book and sprang up from the bench. 'Go away!' she hissed. 'I don't want to talk to you!'

'Hey, don't bite my head off!' I protested. I noticed by the way that Ellie and Geri had niftily slipped out of sight.

'Why are you spying on me?' Shah demanded, hugging the sketch pad to her chest.

'I'm not spying. Anyway, why are you bunking off school?'

Shah's eyes flashed furious sparks. 'I'm not bunking off. Mum knows I'm here!'

I stared right back at her. 'No she doesn't. She thinks you're finishing your art project in Miss Ganeri's room. Skye told me.'

'See; you are spying!'

'Oh, for goodness' sake, Shah, who are you trying to kid? You've screwed up letters to your mum and dad and got away with it, but you never really thought you could carry off this stupid trick, did you?'

95

I was gesturing down the length of the gallery when Shah went nuts. She pushed me back against the bench and I sat down hard. Her sketch book went flying across the polished floor.

Gorilla Man broke into a lumbering trot.

'Get lost, Tiffany!' Shah yelled.

I sprang back to my feet. 'Face it, Shah, you've made a total mess of your life! Mr White knows everything. In fact, he's probably phoning your mum and dad right now!'

G. Man began to lurch forward at a gallop.

Shah was white with fury. 'You told him!' she screeched. Tiffany Little, you dobbed me in!'

That was the last I knew before I got kicked out. That bit's still a blur; except that I eventually landed on the stone step flanked by the giant pillars, with Geri and Ellie looking down at me in total disgust.

Friday, June 1st

Threw mag away, so have no stars to read.

Have just re-read yesterday's entry. So much bad stuff, and it went on until much later in the evening.

5.00 p.m. — rang Mum in tears. Blubbed down
the phone about getting kicked out of
the gallery.

6.00 p.m. — Mum came straight from work to
pick me and Scott up a day early.
Left Dad a note telling him there
was no food in the house so he'd have
to go to Tesco.

7.00 p.m. — Mum heard the full story and
steamed right around to the
Allertons' place. She forced me to
go too.

'I don't care what sort of trouble Fuschia has got
herself into,' my mum told Mrs A. 'There's no
need for her to take it out on Tiff!'

Shah's face was red and puffy, so I was
guessing Mr White must definitely have rung the
Allertons.

Honestly, if looks could kill, I'd have been
stone cold dead on the floor, the way she stared
at me.

'Fuschia, take Tiffany into the telly room while
Gina and I have a chat,' Mrs A said, in a way that
you couldn't argue with.

We didn't watch telly though.

'I thought you were supposed to be my friend!' Shah sobbed. 'How could you dob me in?'

'I didn't!' I yelled back. 'How many times do I have to tell you? I've been doing the best I can to help you, believe it or not!'

She didn't – believe it, that is. Instead, she screwed up her soggy tissues and looked straight at me. 'I hate you, Tiffany Little!' she whispered.

Then she ran upstairs and banged her bedroom door.

I've never been hated before. Except by Scott, and that doesn't count.

I hate being hated. It sucks.

'It's not your fault,' Mum insisted as she handed over the tissues.

I was blubbing over her pale blue sofa. I blubbed most of the night and went into school looking like Elephant Man.

'God, you look awful!' Ellie greeted me. She was dead excited because Heather had heard from Callum's manager, Micky Henderson.

So I took my swollen face into a corner and sulked.

Which is when I spotted Carli and George deep in another of those conversations. They were out in the corridor and I saw and heard them through an open door.

'How about me cooking you a meal tonight?' Carli said, tilting her head up to eyeball him.

'Sounds good,' he said.

'What time?' she said.

'How about eight o'clock?' he said.

'Cool. I'll expect you then,' she said.

This means I wasn't mistaken about them being an item. I feel let down in some weird way, but really it's Dad who's being two-timed, remember.

George arrived ready to teach Romeo and Juliet. The scene near the end where Romeo thinks Juliet is dead and drinks the poison.

Does George know that Carli is cheating on my dad by going out with him? I tried to read his mind as he talked about the tragic passion of Romeo. 'He's a character of great extremes,' he told us. 'Very impulsive, very intense.'

'Just like Chucky Gilbert!' Squealer said.

End of lesson.

A weekend ahead – bummer! Too much time to sit and mope. Can't write, can't read, can't think of anything except being hated by Shah.

Saturday, June 2nd

Your stars – Awww! You're not a happy bunny. But don't worry, your love life is hotting up. It's a great weekend for chillin' and snoggin'.

Mum bought me a new copy of Sugar to cheer me up.

Scott invited Nic round to the flat and they've spent every second so far watching footie.

'No way was that offside! Give the linesman a pair of glasses! Referee!' Nic is acting just like Scott; eating truckloads of Pringles, putting his feet up on the coffee table, nipping out for a pee during the ad breaks. I'm beginning to think he's over Skye.

Hah, so he's watching Sky Sports instead!

Suspect that all 21st century lads lead v. shallow emotional lives. There are no Romeos around any more, ready to drink poison for you.

At about eleven this morning, I heard Mum

take a phone call from Gran. She listened a lot without getting a word in. Then she said, 'Never mind, it's not your fault. I know you meant well. But you know what Ross is like; he hates pressure. Anyway, Mum, it's not that simple, is it?'

'That was your gran saying sorry she stuck her nose in earlier this week,' Mum explained to me afterwards. 'It sounds as if she's still feeling really bad.'

The new news about Carli and George was on the tip of my tongue. I would've blurted it out if there hadn't been a ring on the doorbell and we got our surprise visit of the century.

'D'you have time for a chat?' Mrs Allerton said. She stood in the doorway with Shah, who wasn't red and puffy any more, but pale and strained. Her hair was scraped back, and she was wearing ordinary jeans and T-shirt.

Mum bristled. 'That depends,' she said.

'Shah has something to say to Tiffany.' Mrs A stood to one side and waited.

Shah cleared her throat. 'Tiff, I'm sorry!' she blurted out. 'I know it might not make any difference, and I wouldn't blame you if you never spoke to me again, but I am so sorry!'

I was stunned.

'Listen, I know I made a total mess of everything . . .'

'Stop!' I muttered.

'Come in,' Mum said.

Shah looked nervous as anything.

'Go in.' Mrs A gave her a little shove. 'We've had a heart to heart,' she explained to us. 'A lot of things came out about school and the teachers. I'm afraid Shah didn't handle her problems very well, but from now on we're going to make sure that things are different.'

Mum nodded. 'That's great.'

They talked a bit about how Shah had never found it easy to fit in with school routines.

'She's too much head-in-the-clouds,' was how Mrs A described it. 'And I expect she drives her teachers mad.'

'No everyone is the same,' Mum pointed out. 'Shah has always been a very sensitive, imaginative kid; a bit like Tiff really.'

Sensitive? Imaginative? Me? Is that good or bad?

'Come into my room,' I said to Shah.

I heard her give a big sigh, then she followed me.

'Relax,' I told her.

Colour was flooding back into her cheeks. 'Are we still mates?'

I nodded. 'D'you think I wanna lose you?'

Shah sniffed. 'I was a total cow.'

'Yep.'

'Especially to you.'

I nodded. 'But you were right about Dad and Carli. They were a BIG mistake!' I told her about our two-timing love cheat of an art teacher.

'Your dad's too nice.'

'D'you think I should tell him she's seeing George?'

Shah though hard. 'Nope.'

'OK, I won't.'

'It's weird . . .' Shah paused and stared out of the window. 'I don't know why I blanked you out when I got into a mess. You'd think you'd be the first person I turned to.'

'It was a pride thing,' I guessed.

'Yeah, you're right. I didn't want to admit what was happening. And everyone was on my case – Mr White, Miss Hornby, even Miss Ganeri!'

'Poor you!' Hey, was I glad things were turning out OK. 'I missed you,' I told her.

Shah choked up.

'No blubbing! Hey, and no more weird clothes, OK!'

She smiled through trembling lips.

'And no more candles and Kareena!'

She laughed and agreed to start liking Gemini again.

'Hey, and why don't you show your sketch book to Carli on Monday? I bet she'll be dead impressed!'

Enough emotion for one day, you would have thought.

But no; Dad rang while Mrs A and Mum were

still chatting. 'Tiffany, bad news I'm afraid. Bud has scarpered.'

'What d'you mean?'

'Scarpered, as in run off, legged it, disappeared.'

'Oh no!'

'Worse; he's not wearing his collar.'

'So no name tag?'

'Right. Listen, we'd better set up a search party. Is Scott there with you?'

'Yeah, he's watching footie with Nic.'

'Get them to come home, fast as they can.'

'OK, I'll tell everyone Bud's gone missing,' I promised.

Which I did.

'It's 2-1 to Nigeria!' Scott yelped. 'Ireland is down to ten men. There's forty minutes to go, not counting injury time!'

'This is an emergency!' I yelled, grabbing the remote and switching the telly off.

There was a mini riot, then Nic decided they'd better help.

'C'mon, Mum!' I cried. 'Bud has done a runner!'

He could be anywhere; on the main street, in traffic, getting run over . . .

We all squeezed into Mum and Mrs A's car and hared across to our house.

'Bud's been spotted in the park!' Dad reported. So we raced round here.

'Grab your bikes!' Dad told Scott and me. 'The rest can go on foot!'

Major panic. Total trauma. Bud could be squished under a car.

'Does he do this often?' Shah asked me, before I hopped on my bike.

'Never.' Normally Bud is too lazy to move a muscle unless he's dragged out on the lead. I reckon all the upset of the last week has got to him and sent him screwy . . .

The park was crowded with old men walking dogs, kids playing on the swings and skateboarding.

'Spread out!' Dad ordered. 'Ask everyone if they've seen Bud!'

We worked as a team. 'No, sorry . . . no . . . what kind of dog? . . . no collar? . . . nope . . . no!'

I zoomed around on my bike, over to the duck pond, then coming back full circle. 'Any news?' I yelled at Scott, who was doing 30mph downhill.

'Someone saw him by the ice cream van!' he yelled back.

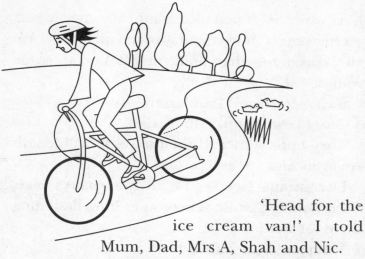

'Head for the
ice cream van!' I told
Mum, Dad, Mrs A, Shah and Nic.

'Yeah, I saw him,' the man in the van told us.
'He nicked an ice cream cone from a guy, then
scarpered.'

We groaned and started calling Bud's name.
Dad whistled.

'Here, Buddy boy!' Mum called. We were all
working together, even Scott.

'There he is!' Nic spotted the runaway
creeping round the back of the hut where they
store the rowing boats for the pond.

Bud was looking dead guilty, with ice cream
smeared all over his face.

'I'll go this way!' Mum ran to cut him off on
the left flank. Dad set off to the right. I followed

him, while Scott pedalled frantically after Mum.

Our pincer movement worked perfectly. We all arrived together and cut off Bud's escape routes.

'Leave it to me!' Dad hissed.

'No, I've got him!' Mum cried.

They both launched themselves in full length rugby tackles . . . and missed.

Bud sprang free – straight into Scott's bike. Scott wobbled and crashed on to him, flattening the poor mutt.

Mum and Dad grabbed thin air, then each other.

'You OK?' Dad gasped.

Mum nodded and pushed her hair out of her eyes.

'Sorry!' Dad pulled her up and dusted her down.

'No, I'm fine, really!'

Their eyes met for the first time in months. Electric moment.

Then they laughed.

'It's not funny!' Scott

was still on the ground, wrestling Bud.

Nic arrived and held the dog in a headlock. Shah and Mrs A found a piece of rope in the hut and made a lead. Then we all went home.

'Enough excitement for one day,' Mum declared. She was making tea in the bombed-out kitchen. Bud was in disgrace. Nic and Scott were re-glued to the telly. '2-2. Nigeria have made a substitution. We're in extra time!'

Mrs A and Shah were planning to leave.

'We'll leave you to it,' Mrs A told us.

'Can Shah stay?' I asked.

So we fixed a sleepover at Mum's place. Shah grinned. I grinned back.

'Here's your tea, Ross.' Mum handed him his favourite mug. I was still grinning.

'Take that look off your face, young lady!' Mum warned. 'Nothing's changed!'

But I'd seen THE MOMENT!

'Actually, something has,' Dad told her.

It was hold-on-to-your-hats time again. He coughed and got tongue-tied.

'There's something I've been meaning to

mention,' he mumbled. 'Carli and I – that is – we – er, well, we decided to call it a day!'

'When?' Gran asked me on the phone.

I rang her the minute we got back to Mum's flat.

'Last Monday, Bank Holiday, in the morning. Dad and Carli decided to be friends, but not an item any more. They agreed it was better.'

'Hm,' Gran said. Then a big pause, during which Gran was thinking, 'What did I tell you! But I'm not going to say, "Told you so!".' The silence was enough.

Mum grabbed the phone from me. 'Don't read too much into it,' she warned Gran.

'Hm,' I heard Gran say again.

'We only bumped into one another; literally, smack and down on the ground! . . . no, it was a complete accident . . . all Bud's fault . . . and yes, I did make tea . . . but that's all . . . yes, at least we're talking again . . . no, not really any plans. We might meet up for a chat some time. Nothing's definite . . . Yes, I can tell you're pleased. Listen, I have to go now, Mum. Bye!'

I was still grinning. What a day. I mean, what a mega day!

Then Geri and Ellie dropped by to take me to town.

They said, 'Gasp – wow! – cool!' when they found Shah and me in my room, buddy-buddies again.

'Eng-land! Eng-land!' Scott and Nic chanted next door.

'C'mon, let's go!' Ellie said. Like me, she was so over Nic!

Explanations could come later, Geri said, after they'd dragged me down to the art gallery café.

'There's this cute lad working there,' Ellie reported. 'We saw him the other day. I decided right away that he was your type, Tiff. So Geri and me popped in earlier today and chatted him up for you.'

'You did what?' I squealed.

'His name's Damion. He's shy but cute,' Geri explained. 'You're really gonna like him, Tiff; honest!'

'What did you tell him?' I yelled, as they dragged me kicking and screaming between the two stone pillars. 'Wait! Hang on! Don't do this to me!'

The naked statue stared down. Ellie froofed

up my hair, Geri propelled me towards the café.

Shah giggled. 'Go for it, Tiff!' she whispered.

Yep, Café Boy was well cool – tall and skinny, short, dark hair, great eyes. I always go by the eyes.

So I took a deep breath (Here Comes the Future), straightened my top, stuck out my chest and ordered a Coke . . .